Mix the shapes up,
move them around
and they RESHAPE!

These shapes reshape
into BUZZY things!

What could they be?

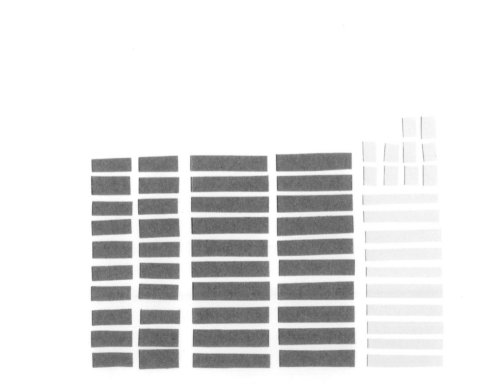

10 DRAGONFLIES,
flittering and fluttering.

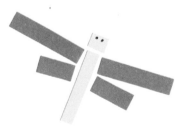

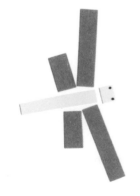

These shapes reshape
into JUMPY things!

What could they be?

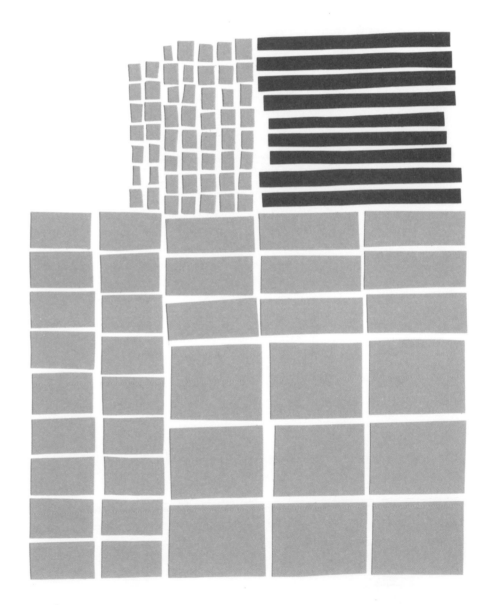

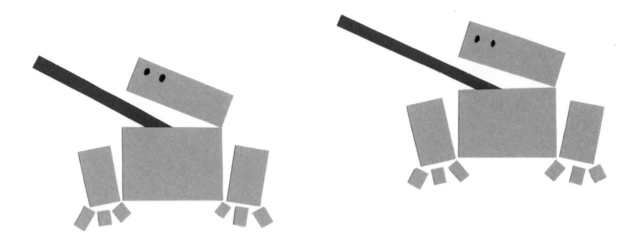

9 FROGS,
slimy and slurping.

These shapes reshape
into STRIPY things!

What could they be?

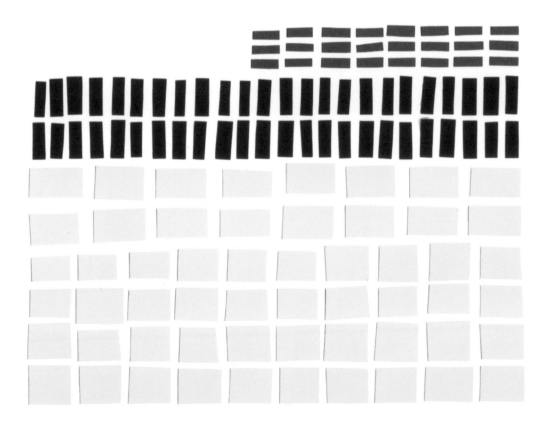

8 SNAKES,
sneakily slithering.

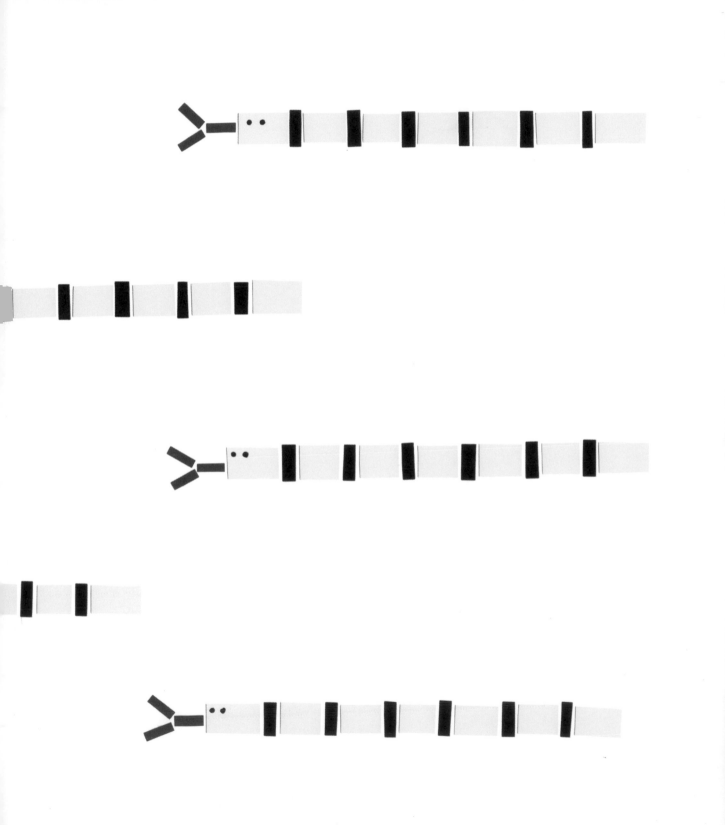

These shapes reshape
into CLUCKY things!

What could they be?

7 **CHICKENS,**
peck, peck, pecking.

These shapes reshape
into PRICKLY things!

What could they be?

6 **HEDGEHOGS,**
sniffly and snuffling.

These shapes reshape
into PINCHY things!

What could they be?

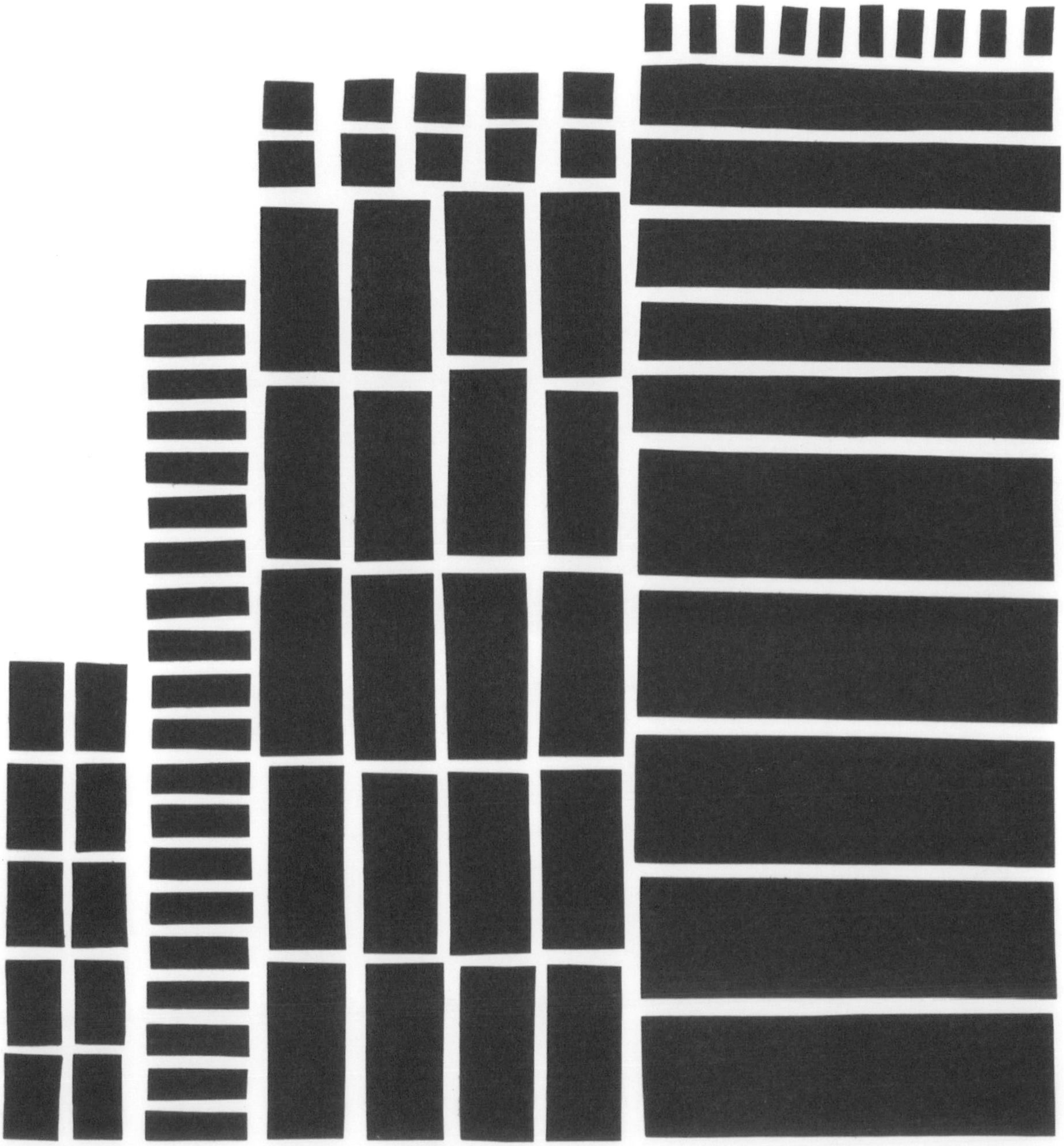

5 CRABS,
nip-your-nose nipping.

These shapes reshape
into ROARY things!

What could they be?

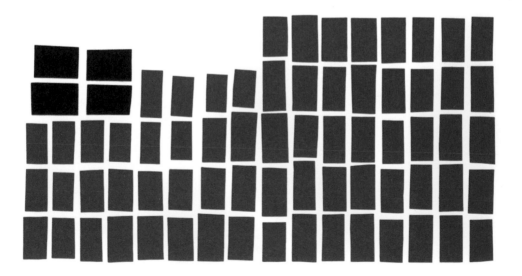

4 **LIONS,**
hungry and hunting.

These shapes reshape
into SCALY things!

What could they be?

3 **ALLIGATORS,**
snip, snap, snapping.

These shapes reshape
into STOMPY things!

What could they be?

2 RHINOCEROSES,
stamping and stampeding.

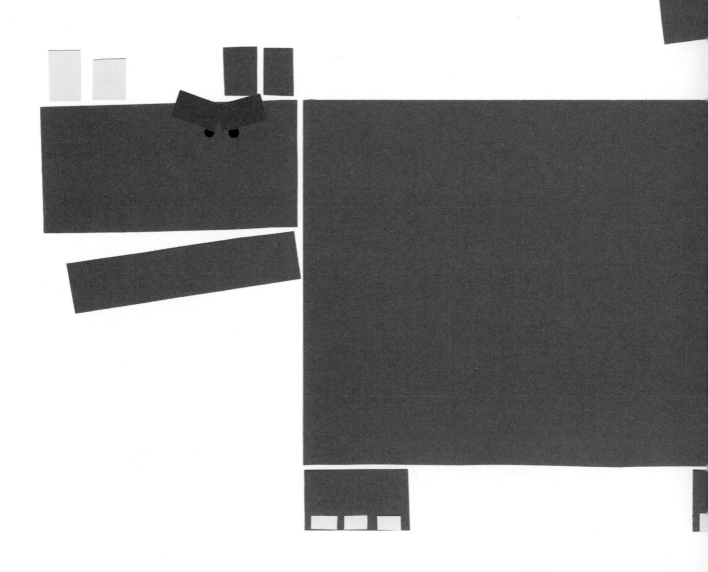

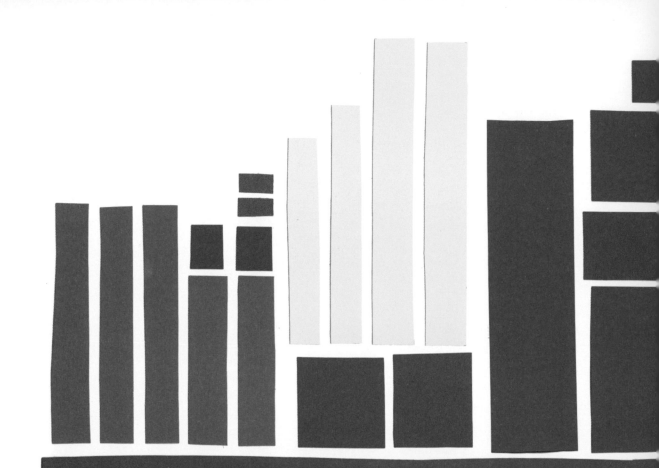

These shapes reshape
into a FIERY thing!

What could it be?

1 DRAGON,
fearsome and fire-breathing.

But not for long ...

because something scared the dragon!

What could it possibly be?

A spider,
teeny-weeny and oh so tiny!